As You Like It

Sweet Cherry
Publishing

Published by Sweet Cherry Publishing Limited
Unit E, Vulcan Business Complex,
Vulcan Road,
Leicester, LE5 3EB,
United Kingdom

First published in the USA in 2013
ISBN: 978-1-78226-068-4

©Macaw Books

Title: As You Like It
North American Edition

Text & Illustration by Macaw Books 2013

www.sweetcherrypublishing.com

Printed and bound by Wai Man Book Binding (China) Ltd. Kowloon, H.K.

About Shakespeare

William Shakespeare, regarded as the greatest writer in the English language, was born in Stratford-upon-Avon in Warwickshire, England (around April 23, 1564). He was the third of eight children born to John and Mary Shakespeare.

Shakespeare was a poet, playwright, and dramatist. He is often known as England's national poet and the "Bard of Avon." Thirty-eight plays, 154 sonnets, two long narrative poems, and several other poems are attributed to him. Shakespeare's plays have been translated into every major existent language and are performed more often than those of any other playwright.

Duke Frederick: He has usurped his brother, Duke Senior, from the dukedom. He is cruel and has an awful temper. He also banishes Rosalind to the Forest of Arden due to his hatred for her father.

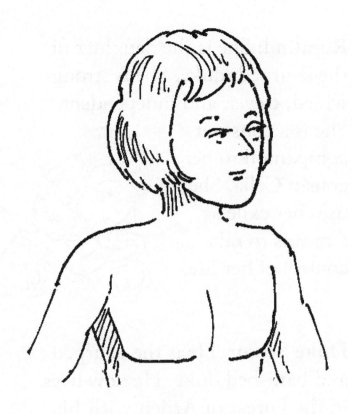

Orlando: He is a handsome young man who has had no education or training. However, he proves himself to be a gentleman when he takes care of his aging servant, protects his brother from a lioness, and wins the wrestling match.

Rosalind: She is the daughter of the usurped, duke. She is strong-willed, clever, and independent. She is a constant companion to her cousin Celia. She uses her exile as a means to take control of her life.

Duke Senior: He is the usurped and banished duke. He now lives in the Forest of Arden with his counselors. He is kindhearted and generous. He lives in the forest, content, happy, and celebrating life.

As You Like It

There was a small kingdom in France ruled by a usurper—a man who had taken the throne away from its rightful owner, his elder brother, and had then banished him.

The banished duke, having nothing left to call his own, decided to take refuge in the nearby Forest of Arden. But as happens with all noblemen, the duke's courtiers decided to go with him to the forest and stay with him during his period of exile. They lived there like Robin Hood and his Merry Men. They

found new ways of
amusing themselves
and making merry,
reciting poetry
and talking about
how the winter
winds, though cold
and harsh, were
better than men
who appeared to be friendly
but stabbed you in the back.

Now, the banished duke
had a daughter called Rosalind.
Duke Frederick, the usurper,
when banishing his elder brother,
did not allow Rosalind to go
with him, as he wanted her to
remain as a companion to his
own daughter, Celia. The young

girls were great friends and not once did they let the relationship between their fathers affect them.

Celia knew of the injustice that had been meted out to Rosalind, and whenever her friend was upset and remembered her father, Celia would try to cheer her up. One day, Celia was trying to cheer up her friend Rosalind

when suddenly, a messenger from
the duke arrived and informed
the girls that a wrestling match
was about to start, and if they
were interested, they could
come along and watch it. Celia
immediately thought that this
would take Rosalind's mind off
her misery and agreed to go.

However, when they reached the wrestling pit, what they saw failed to amuse them. A huge man was about to wrestle with a thin young man, who looked rather inexperienced. The duke

summoned the two girls and
asked them to talk to this young
lad and beg him to pull out of
the fight before he was killed.

Celia and Rosalind immediately
agreed to do this good deed

and went over to the man. First, Celia tried to persuade him, but when Rosalind spoke to him, her words had a different effect. Far from walking away from the fight, he now wanted to prove his worth to this beautiful lady, and he calmly remarked, "I am sorry to deny such fair and excellent ladies anything. If I am killed, there is one dead who is willing to die; I shall do my friends no wrong, for I have none to lament me."

Soon the wrestling match started. Celia prayed for the young man to come out of the

ordeal unhurt, but Rosalind
was pained by the young man's
words of death and how he
was friendless in this world.
She found his situation as
unfortunate as her own, and
at that moment, she fell in
love with the young wrestler.

However, in the wrestling pit, a different story was unfolding. Encouraged by the kind words of the two ladies, the young wrestler was starting to overcome the giant. Within minutes, the match was over and the young man stood over his opponent victorious. Duke Frederick wanted to know

the name of the young man and about his family so that he could take him under his protection.

The young man replied that his name was Orlando and that he was the youngest son of the now deceased Sir Rowland de Boys. Duke Frederick was most upset upon hearing this, because it was a known fact that Sir Rowland de Boys had been a great admirer of his elder brother, the banished duke. His appreciation for the youth turned hostile and he simply remarked, "I wish you had been the son of any other man."

Rosalind, though, was delighted to hear about Orlando's

lineage. It made her feel closer to him, learning that their fathers had been good friends. As the duke left, Rosalind and Celia immediately went up to Orlando and started to converse. Before leaving, Rosalind took off her gold chain and gave it to Orlando to remember her by.

When the two girls were
alone in their chambers, Rosalind
could not stop talking about
Orlando. Sensing something
brewing in Rosalind's heart for
the gallant man, Celia asked
her whether she was in love

with him. Rosalind merely
replied that she was fond
of him because his
father had been a good
friend of her own
father. To that Celia
remarked, "But does
it therefore follow
that you should
love his son dearly?
For then I ought
to hate him, for
my father hated his father;
yet I do not hate Orlando!"

Meanwhile, Frederick
was enraged at having met Sir
Rowland de Boys's son, and
being reminded of his elder
brother and all his well-wishers

who had followed the rightful
duke to the forest rather than
be members of Frederick's court.
His anger was soon directed
toward Rosalind, who now
more than ever reminded him

of her father. So while the girls were talking about Orlando, Duke Frederick stormed into the room and ordered Rosalind to leave his house. Celia tried to intervene, but her father's orders were irreversible.

When Celia realized that her unjust father would not change his mind, she decided to go with  Rosalind to the forest, leaving the house that very night.

But there was one problem. They realized that it would be unsafe for them to venture into the forest alone, so Rosalind decided to dress as a boy while Celia would pretend to be a simple country lass. They would say that they were brother and sister, which would keep them safe in the forest. Rosalind took the name Ganymede and Celia called herself Aliena.

Finally, the two girls were ready to leave the house. They took as much money and jewels as they could lay their hands on. They walked a long way before they finally reached the Forest of Arden. It was only then that the two girls, now brother and sister, realized how arduous the road

ahead would be, for there would be no more inns for them to stay at and nowhere to get food.

Celia, or Aliena as she was now called, was so tired that

she refused to walk any farther.
Rosalind, or rather Ganymede,
was also very tired, but she
could not show it because she
was supposed to be a man!

Finally, after many agonizing
moments, they met a poor little
shepherd boy passing the same
way. Ganymede, in his most

manly voice, asked the shepherd
if he knew of a small house
they could stay in, to which the
shepherd replied that his own
master's house was just about to
be sold, and perhaps Ganymede
and his sister could purchase it.
So he led them to the house in
the village, which they bought

along with some supplies, and the shepherd stayed on as an errand boy. They moved into the house and decided to start looking for the duke the next day.

In the meantime, there were certain developments in the town. Orlando, son of the deceased Sir Rowland de Boys, was having problems of his own. His elder brother, Oliver, who was left in charge of taking care of him, had given him no attention his whole life. Far from

enrolling him in a school, Oliver did not even bother to stop his brother from taking part in wrestling matches. That was why Orlando had confided in Rosalind about how he had nothing to live for and that no one would even mourn his death.

Oliver had learned of Orlando's heroic feat at the wrestling match

that day, but instead of being proud of his brother's success, he could not help feeling the pangs of jealousy. So he decided that at night, when Orlando was asleep, he would set fire to his room.

But as always happens to evil-doers, an old servant of the house

overheard Oliver's plans. He was loyal to Sir Rowland de Boys and was also very fond of Orlando, so when Orlando came home that evening, he told him about Oliver's plan and begged the boy to run away. He gave him all the money he had saved while working for Sir Rowland de

Boys, and asked Orlando to take him with him, because he did not want to be left alone with Oliver.

Without wasting any time, Orlando and his faithful servant left for the Forest of Arden, where they thought they would

be safe. But once they were in the forest, Orlando realized that the servant's money would be of no use to him. There was nowhere he could buy food, and so he decided to leave his tired servant in a shady grove and go in search of something to eat. Though he walked for quite some distance, he found nothing.

Suddenly, Orlando heard voices and started walking in that direction. He saw that there was a small crowd gathered, settling down to have dinner. Being unable to resist all the tempting

food that was before him,
Orlando drew his sword and
jumped before the party, yelling,
"Out with it…all your food!"

It was actually the old duke
and his banished ministers,
who were just about to start
their meal. The duke looked

quizzically at Orlando and
told him that they were not
savages and he was welcome to
join them for something to
eat. But Orlando said that he
had an old companion with
him, and he would not touch
a morsel until he was fed. So
the duke asked some of his

men to go with Orlando and bring back his friend. Slowly Orlando's old faithful servant regained his strength.

Now that all was well between the duke and Orlando, the duke asked the

young man who he was and what
he was doing in the forest. When
he learned Orlando's identity, he
immediately took him under his
protection. From that day on,
Orlando and his old servant were
part of the duke's entourage.

One day,
in the forest,
Ganymede was
surprised to see
Rosalind's name
carved on the
tree trunks. The
whole forest was
full of her name.
The brother and
sister also found
several love
sonnets marked on the various
trees where Rosalind's name
was carved. While
they were still
trying to guess
who could be the
master of such

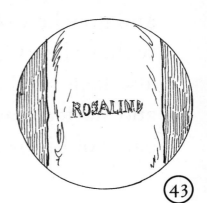

work, they stumbled upon Orlando. Ganymede saw that the gold chain she had given him when she was the fair Rosalind was still around his neck.

The three became friends. Orlando, of course, did not know that Ganymede was actually the lovely Rosalind who had stolen his heart, so he kept telling him about the woman of his dreams, and how he would die without her. Ganymede also kept up the pretense and started playing a little game of his own. He told

Orlando that he had a certain
plan which would surely solve
all his problems. He asked
Orlando to come to his cottage
every day, where he must try
to woo the noble Ganymede,
who would pretend that he was

Rosalind and would thwart all of Orlando's attempts. Ganymede was certain that Orlando would soon forget all about Rosalind.

However, when the game began, it did not look as if Ganymede would be successful.

Orlando came to Ganymede's house every day and played the game of make-believe. Even though this exercise did not make him forget his love for Rosalind, it did give him an opportunity to say what he felt in his heart. And this also helped Ganymede, as Rosalind, to confirm her love for Orlando.

While pursuing the matters of his own heart, Ganymede made no attempt to let his father know who he really was. Learning

about the duke from Orlando,
Ganymede did go to meet him

once, but he refrained from
telling him who he was, because
he saw that his father was very
happy in his new surroundings.

One fine morning, as
Orlando made his way to
Ganymede's house, he saw his
brother, Oliver, lying by a tree,
asleep. Suddenly, he saw that a

lioness was sitting close by, ready
to pounce on Oliver when he
awoke. First, Orlando thought
about leaving his cruel brother
to his fate, but soon brotherly
affection overwhelmed him and
he started to fight with the lioness.
During the scuffle, Oliver awoke
to find that his brother was trying

to save him at the cost of his own life. But before Orlando could slay the lion, the hungry animal managed to injure his arm. Oliver immediately tried to nurse his brother back to health, and the two brothers were reconciled.

Orlando asked his brother
to go to the house of Ganymede
to tell him that he would not
be able to come because of
his injury. Oliver immediately

went and told Ganymede
everything that had happened.
He also introduced himself as
Orlando's elder brother and
told them the whole story.
Ganymede and Aliena were
content to know that the two
brothers were now reunited.

The genuine sorrow that
Oliver felt for his brother and

about their past relationship had
a deep impact on Aliena. She
immediately fell in love with
Oliver, and Oliver could not help
but stare at the pretty Aliena
and also fell in love with her.

But as Ganymede was told
about Orlando's fatal injury, he
collapsed to the ground. This made
Oliver wonder about Ganymede,

as no man would faint upon hearing such news. On recovering, Ganymede made up a story about how he was pretending to be Rosalind and therefore acted as if he had fainted, but Oliver was not convinced.

He went back to Orlando and told him about Ganymede

collapsing, and how he had fallen in love with Aliena. He went on to say that if they were to get married, he would stay with his beloved Aliena in the forest and live like a simple shepherd for the rest of his life.

Orlando immediately arranged for the marriage to be held the

next day. He even went to the
duke and invited him and all
his ministers to the wedding.
Later that day, when Orlando
met Ganymede, he told him
about his wish to be married
to Rosalind the same day as
Aliena and Oliver were to get
married. Ganymede told him

that if such were the desire
in his heart, he would see to
it that Rosalind came to the
wedding and married Orlando.

Orlando readily agreed
to Ganymede's proposal. He
went and told the duke about
the whole episode and both
waited for the next day to come

so that they could once again
see their beloved Rosalind.

The next day
was the day of the
wedding between
Aliena and Oliver.
The duke and
Orlando were
anxiously waiting
to see a miracle
happen, and it
soon did. Instead
of Ganymede and
Aliena, Rosalind
and Celia arrived.
The duke and
Orlando were
overjoyed to see
Rosalind, who
wasted no time
in telling both

the men everything they had
done since leaving home.

While all the people in the
Forest of Arden were reconciling
with one another, a messenger
arrived from the city. He said
that Duke Frederick had given up
on his claim to the dukedom and

left it for his elder brother, to whom it rightfully belonged.

They were informed that after his daughter ran away and came to the forest, Frederick had grown more livid toward his banished elder brother. In fact, he was on his way to the forest with a huge army to kill everyone when he met a hermit, who told him he was making a huge mistake.

From that moment, he decided to give up his dukedom.

So it was finally a rather happy moment for all the people present. The duke got his dukedom back, Orlando and Rosalind were married, Oliver and Celia were married, and Orlando and Oliver were reconciled. It was a great day in the Forest of Arden.